KEYBOARD   Compiled and edited by Gail Smith

CREATIVE KEYBOARD PRESENTS
J. S. BACH COLLECTION
Book One

Visit us on the Web at http://www.melbay.com — E-mail us at email@melbay.com

CREATIVE KEYBOARD PUBLICATIONS • P.O. BOX 66 • PACIFIC, MO 63069-0066

BOOK ONE
TABLE OF CONTENTS

JOHANN SEBASTIAN BACH
CHRONOLOGY

		Age	
March 21,	1685		Born at Eisenach, where his father, Johann Ambrosius Bach, was Court and Town musician. From his father he learned the violin.
May,	1694	(9)	His mother, Elizabeth, died.
January,	1695	(10)	His father died; the orphaned boy and his brother Jakob then went to Ohrdruf to live with their elder brother, Johann Christoph, who taught him to play the clavichord.
March,	1700	(15)	Set out for Lüneberg, two hundred miles distant, where his fine treble voice procured him a livelihood in the choir of St. Michael's Convent. Here his earliest compositions were put on paper.
April,	1703	(18)	Became Court violinist at Weimar.
August,	1703	(18)	Installed as organist in the New Church at Arnstadt.
October,	1705	(20)	Obtained four weeks' leave of absence and walked all the way to Lübeck to hear the famous Buxtehude. He stayed until February, 1706, was greatly influenced by this master, and was duly reprimanded upon his tardy return to Arnstadt.
June 15,	1707	(22)	Appointed organist at Mühlhausen.
October 17,	1707	(22)	Married his cousin, Maria Barbara Bach.

WEIMAR (1708-1717)

July,	1708	(23)	Removed to Weimar as Court organist and violinist to Duke Wilhelm Ernst.
March, 2	1714	(29)	Promoted to be Konzertmeister at Weimar.

CÖTHEN (1717-1723)

December 10,	1717	(32)	Began as Kapellmeister to Prince Leopold of Anhalt at Cöthen.
July,	1720	(35)	During his absence at Carlsbad, his wife died.
December, 3	1721	(36)	Married Anna Magdalena Wülken, a beautiful singer.

LEIPZIG (1723-1750)

June 1,	1723	(38)	Installed as cantor of the Thomasschule, Leipzig, and as organist and director of music at both the Thomaskirche and the Nicolaikirche.
August,	1741	(56)	Visited Berlin. His second son, Carl Philipp Emanuel, had been appointed cembalist to Frederick the Great in 1740.
May,	1747	(62)	In response to repeated expressions of Frederick's desire, he visited Potsdam with his son Wilhelm Friedemann. A summons brought him at once to the Court, where he played on Frederick's new Silbermann pianofortes and improvised at length for the King.
	1749	(65)	Because of failing eyesight his eyes were twice operated upon, resulting in total blindness. Ten days before his death his eyesight returned.
July 28,	1750	(66)	Succumbed to apoplexy and fever.
July 31,	1750	(66)	Buried in an unmarked grave near the south door of the Johanniskirche. In 1885 a tablet was placed on the south wall of the church. His wife and three unmarried daughters were left in poverty and became dependent on town charity.

FOREWORD

The music of Johann Sebastian Bach is timeless. He was a master composer whose music is used today as a model for all serious composers. Bach's music is both divine and difficult.

This series of five books begins with Bach's easiest piece, the *Minuet in G* and ends with his monumental work, *The Goldberg Variations*.

All the selections have been carefully chosen for their variety and charm. All the popular pieces from the *Notebook for Anna Magdalena; Little Preludes & Fugues*; selections from the *Well-Tempered Clavier Vol 1. and 2*; Two-part Inventions, Three-part Inventions, French and English Suites, Partitas, Toccatas, Chromatic Fantasy and Italian Concerto have been included. The five books contain a perfect collection of Bach for the serious pianist.

While working on this series, scores of editions have been carefully analyzed. Editions edited by Dr. William Mason have been used as well as editions edited by Carl Czerny. Special care has been taken on the preludes and fugues to delete the false mix and match that the Buonamici editions included. Buonamici actually changed the keys of several of Bach's fugues and joined them with other preludes on his own whim. Here is what he said in his edition of *Eighteen Little Preludes and Fugues*, "I have also to claim indulgence for the slight license taken in transposing preludes Nos. 5, 11, and 13 a tone." You may be assured that none of those assorted Preludes and Fugues are in this series, only the actual six that Bach composed and joined together.

The interpretation and use of embellishments as prescribed by Bach are included along with a short biography with pictures and a chronology of the life and music of Johann Sebastian Bach.

How wonderful it would be if we could hear a recording of Bach playing Bach. What a treasure we have with the amount of his works available to play on the piano today. We'll never know what music of Bach's was lost to this world, but what remains is a challenge to any pianist.

Gail Smith

The greatest composer of all time was Johann Sebastian Bach. Robert Schumann might have said it best, "to whom music owes almost as great a debt as a religion owes to its founder."

Bach was born on March 21, 1685 in the small German town of Eisenach. Throughout two centuries the Bach family was known for their musical talent. Bach's father, Johann Ambrosius Bach (1645-1695) was the court and town musician as well as a violinist and organist. Bach's mother was Elizabeth Lammerhirt of Erfurt. Bach's parents died when he was just nine years old. Being the youngest child in the family, it was decided that Johann Sebastian would move to Ohrdruf and live with Christoph, his older brother who had recently married and had a position as organist there. Christoph was born on June 16, 1671 and studied with the famous Pachelbel.

At the age of five Bach was taught to play the violin by his father. While living with his brother Christoph, Bach quickly learned to play the clavier also. Soon Bach could play just as well as his older brother. The story is told that young Bach's brother refused to let him play from a certain book of clavier pieces by the most famous composers of the day. The cabinet that Christoph kept the music book in had a simple lattice front that Bach could reach his hand into. Finally the temptation was too great and Bach began pulling the music out secretly at night and copied it by moonlight, sometimes staying up all night. The task of copying the music took at least six months. One day however, when Bach was playing the music from his forbidden book, his brother discovered what Bach had done and took away the music he had copied so carefully.

St. Michael's Church, Ohrdruf

On March 15, 1700, Bach moved from his brother's home in Ohrdruf. He was accepted as a choir boy in Lüneburg where he hoped to finish his studies in the school of the convent of St. Michael. He received free room and board there. Soon however, his voice changed but he was allowed to stay and played several instruments at the school. Later, his first paid position was as a violinist in the orchestra of Duke Johann Ernst.

On July 13, 1703, the town of Weimar recorded that Johann Sebastian Bach arrived to become the organist to the Princely Court of Saxe. He had been asked to inspect and christen the new organ which had been built for the new church. Bach's reputation as a fine organist was growing. He was only eighteen years old and was making a good salary playing the organ for church services. Bach was also in charge of training and directing the church choir. He composed an Easter cantata which his choir performed in 1704. Bach also composed a Capriccio on the departure of his brother Johann Jakob, who had enrolled as a musician in the army of Charles XII about this same time.

In October of 1705 Bach was given a four week leave of absence. He walked twenty-five miles to Lubeck to hear the famous organist Buxtehude play at St. Mary's Church. Bach was dazzled and stayed until February, enjoying the wonderful music he heard. When he returned home, he was severely scolded for having exceeded his leave of absence by three months. Bach was given a week to think things over. He was also accused of playing preludes that were too long. Other charges had been brought up including why he allowed a young woman to sit on the organ bench with him. On June 29, 1707, Bach approached the council, handed them the organ key and asked for his release.

On October 17, 1707, Bach married Maria Barbara, daughter of Michael Bach, organist of Gehren. The marriage took place in the Church of Dornheim near Arnstadt.

Bach was soon appointed organist to the Church of St. Blasius in Muhlhausen. Bach was requested to compose a cantata according to the town custom for the re-election of the town council each year. Bach wrote the cantata, *Gottistmein Konig* for the Change of Council of February 4, 1708. It was in fact the only cantata printed during his lifetime.

On June 25, 1708 Bach handed in his notice at Muhlhausen because the Duke of Saxe-Weimar wanted him to work for him. This was a happy move for Bach since the Councilors of the Muhlhausen Church hadn't appreciated his embellishments, saying Bach's music was "carnal," since it seduced the ear.

At Weimar, Bach was able to escape all religious disputes. The Duke was a patron of the arts and had built an open theatre in 1696. Concerts were given by sixteen musicians dressed in Hungarian costume. The Duke especially enjoyed organ music. Bach composed the majority of his organ works while at Weimar.

Bach became the Kappellmeister for Prince Leopold of Cöthen. Leopold was a very musical prince who played several instruments and had a well-trained voice. Bach's duties were confined to chamber music. These few years at Cöthen were very pleasant. However, after being there just three years, his wife Marie Barbara suddenly

The keyboards of Bach's Arnstadt Organ

died. They had been married for thirteen years. At the time of her death, Bach was away on a journey to Carlsbad with the Prince. When he returned, she had already been buried. They had seven children. During this same year, Bach made the trip to Hamburg and applied for the post of organist there. Another organist, Mr. Heitmann wanted the post and promised 4000 marks to the church if he was appointed organist. The councilors preferred the money to the master organist, Bach. The preacher of the church did not approve of the decision and in his Christmas sermon he referred to the music of angels at Bethlehem and ended his sermon with these words, "If one of these angels descended from heaven to be organist at St. James's and played divinely, but arrived without money, he would be obliged to take flight again."

In 1717, Jean Louis Marchand, the organist for Louis XV was visiting Dresden. Bach was summoned to challenge him. It was to be the Frenchman against the German Bach. Bach agreed to the contest which included sight reading anything put before him and improvising on a theme. Bach arrived at the appointed time but Marchand must have anticipated defeat because he never showed up!

Wing of the Ducal Castle at Cöthen

Bach married Anna Magdalena on December 3, 1721. She was twenty-one years old. Bach was then thirty-six. Anna Magdalena's father was court trumpeter at Weissenfels, and she was a court singer with a beautiful soprano voice. Anna Magdalena was a skilled and patient music copyist and also an accompanist on the clavier. On her twenty-fourth birthday (September 22, 1725), Bach presented her with a beautiful green leather notebook with her initials imprinted in gold on the cover. Inside were many songs he composed for her. They had a very happy marriage. Most evenings there were family concerts in the living room. Anna Magdalena helped Bach copy most of his music including all of the St. Matthew Passion, of which there are a great many parts.

*Johann Sebastian Bach
(From portrait by Hausmann)*

Bach continued his job at Cöthen but things began to change soon after the Prince married Princess Bernburg. She despised music and soon the Prince's fine taste for music disappeared. The Bach children were growing up and the two eldest sons were very talented at the keyboard and showed an interest in composing music. Bach wanted his sons to get a good education. He wanted them to attend the University in Leipzig. When Bach heard that the post of cantor at St. Thomas School in Leipzig was vacant because of the death of Johann Kuhnau, he decided to apply for that position. He applied in December, and in February he auditioned by conducting a cantata there. There were six candidates for the position including the famous composer Telemann who decided not to accept the post because the job of cantor included teaching Latin lessons. Finally Bach was accepted by the town council on May 5, 1723 and ceremoniously admitted into the school on May 31st. There were speeches by the town council delegates and singing by the pupils of St. Thomas.

St. Thomas's School, Leipzig

St. Thomas's Church, Leipzig

Bach and his family were housed in the south wing of the school. Their windows overlooked the river that flowed beneath the wall, upon the mill, the promenade, fields and farms. They lived there twenty-seven years. Bach's salary was 700 thalers a year.

Bach had seven children from his first marriage with Maria Barbara. Three of them survived their father–the eldest daughter, Katharina Dorothea (1708-1774); Wilhelm Friedemann (1710-1784), who at the time was musical director and organist at Halle; and Carl Philipp Emmanuel (1714-1788), Kammer Musikus to the King of Prussia.

Anna Magdalena Wülken bore thirteen children. The eldest of the sons was Gottfried Heinrich (1724-1763). Elizabeth Juliane Friederike in 1749 married one of Bach's pupils, Johann Christoph Altnikol. Their other children were Johann Christoph Friedrich (1732-1795), Johann Christian (1735-1782), the "London Bach," and two daughters, Johanna Caroline (1737-1781) and Regine Susanne (1742-1809). The other children died at an early age. During his lifetime, Bach taught his children as well as approximately 80 private students to play instruments. All authorities agree that Bach was a great teacher and we have a detailed description of his methods in an existing account by one of his students, Heinrich Nikolaus Gerber. Gerber states that

at his first lesson with Bach he was given the inventions to practice, next many of the Suites, then the *Well-Tempered Clavier*. "This work Bach played through three times to him with unapproachable art," Gerber states in his book. When Bach taught a new beginner, he kept the student on finger exercises usually from six to twelve months. When the student lost patience, Bach gave them little pieces, such the six little preludes and the two-part-inventions. He would compose these little pieces during the lesson and make them suit the particular needs and ability of the pupil. Bach always played the piece through and said, "That is how it must sound."

The Bach Family

Probably Bach's most famous student was Johann Goldberg, who played clavier for Count Kayserling, an insomniac. Johann Goldberg was employed to play the harpsichord each evening to help the Count relax and sleep. Goldberg asked Bach if he would compose some special pieces for him to play for Count Kayserling on those sleepless nights. Bach ended up composing thirty pieces. The soothing music delighted Count Kayserling, who paid a generous fee of 100 gold louis d'or for "his variations." They are known today as *The Goldberg Variations*.

Bach was helpful in working on a new system of tuning instruments called "Equal-Temperament." This system made it possible to play in all twelve keys. The old system adhered to intonation according to the natural harmonic series for the more common scales. The extreme sharp and C sharp and flat keys sounded terribly out of tune. F sharp and C sharp, for instance, which were correct according to the natural scale for the keys of G major and D major, could not be used as G flat and D flat in relation to other notes of the G flat major scale. B flat could not be used as A sharp. The principle of the system of equal temperament was to make a slight adjustment between all the chromatic notes in such a way that the intervals were exactly the same relation to each other. Bach had 10 claviers in his home and was able to tune one in just fifteen minutes. Bach was admired in Leipzig and no musician ever came to that city without visiting "the master."

In May, 1747, on the invitation of King Frederick the Great, Bach and his eldest son Friedemann went to Potsdam to visit Carl Phillip Emanuel Bach who was a court musician for the King. When they arrived the King was just about to play his usual flute solo at the evening concert. Bach apologized for appearing in his traveling attire, but the King had summoned them immediately when they arrived in town. The King was excited to meet Bach and took him on a tour of the castle. Bach was impressed with the King's fifteen new Silverman pianofortes. The King played his melody on the flute and Bach improvised a fugue for him. When Bach finally returned back home he wrote out the new fugue and it is known as *The Musical Offering*.

Bach suffered from failing eyesight most of his adult life. Finally he was persuaded to have an operation performed by Dr. Taylor, an English opthalmiater. This doctor had recently performed eye surgery on the famous composer Handel. Instead of helping Bach's failing eyesight, the operation resulted in his becoming totally blind. Bach continued to compose on days when he felt strong, dictating the music to his pupil Johann Muthel. It had been six months since the operation and Bach was becoming weaker and weaker.

On July 18, 1750, Bach suddenly regained his eyesight and seemed to acquire a new lease on life. He had been working on a new chorale with his son-in-law Altnikol writing it down. These are the words to his last chorale, "Before thy throne, my God, I stand. Myself, my all, are in thy hand. Turn to me thine approving face. Nor from me now withhold thy grace. I will appear." Bach died ten days later on Tuesday evening, a quarter past nine, July 28, 1750. The following Friday morning, July 31, Bach was buried in the cemetery of St. John's Church.

Bach was greatly mourned. The great musician Telemann wrote an obituary in verse: "Departed Bach! Long since thy splendid organ playing alone brought thee the noble cognomen 'the Great', and what thy pen had writ, the highest art displaying. Did some with joy and some with envy contemplate. Then sleep! The candle of thy fame ne're low will burn. The pupils thou hast trained and those they train in turn prepare thy future crown of glory brightly glowing. Thy children's hands adore it with its jewels bright, but what shall cause thy true worth to be judged aright Berlin to us now in a worthy son is showing."

Anna Magdalena supported herself until 1760 and then had to live on charity. She gave the Council of Leipzig a motet, three passions, and some cantatas so that they would allow her to continue living at the St. Thomas' School. By the autumn of 1756, only thirty copies of the Art of Fugue had been sold. This was not very encouraging. The eldest son Friedemann soon sold the series of cantatas he had been given as an inheritance. He moved to Berlin and taught piano lessons. There are conflicting stories as to the identity of one of his students. Her name is Sara Levy. Some sources say she was Mendelssohn's grandmother and other sources say she was his great-aunt. Somehow Mendelssohn acquired copies of Bach's music and this is a possible explanation for Mendelssohn's great interest in reviving the music of Bach.

Carl Phillip Emmanuel took much care of the cantatas he received. He chose not to sell them, but instead loaned his scores out for a fee to copy them. When Emmanuel died, his wife carried on the business; when she died the granddaughter of Johann Sebastian Bach announced in the obituary notice that she would continue the business carried on by her late mother with the music of her late father and grandfather.

The youngest daughter Regina Susanna, had a life of hardship. She was just eight years old when her father died. An urgent appeal was made in 1800 by Mr. Rochlitz who was an editor and wrote articles about Bach. He made it known that Bach's only surviving daughter was in need and the public responded. When Beethoven heard of the need he sent in a contribution. The following year Beethoven gave one of his composi- tions to his publisher, Breitkopf and Hartel, instructing them to share the profits of the work with Regina. Beethoven had become acquainted with the music of Bach through his piano teacher, Christian Gottlob Neefe (1748-1798). When Beethoven was a boy he studied the *Well-Tempered Clavichord* composed by Bach.

Bach's music is timeless. Albert Schweitzer said his music was "intoxicating." The amount of music he composed is unbelievable. All the sets of preludes and fugues in every key; the two-part inventions, the

The Monument at Eisenach

three-part inventions; several hundred cantatas. Bach put the initials SDG on the bottom of each song he composed. When asked what that meant he stated that it stood for *Soli Deo Gloria* (To God alone be glory.) Bach stated that "the music doesn't disappear, but the notes ascend to the very throne of God as praise too deep for utterance."

To mark the one hundreth anniversary of his death, the Bach Society was founded in Leipzig. Robert Schumann was one of the original members. Its purpose was to issue all the works of Bach that could be found and print at least one volume annually. In March, 1829 Mendelssohn conducted the St. Matthews Passion in Berlin, one hundred years after its first production. Soon a monument of Bach was erected in Leipzig. Then in 1884, in Eisenach, Bach's birthplace, a monument was erected. At the unveiling of this monument Bach's last descendent, a grandson, Wilhelm Friedmann Ernst Bach, was present with his wife and two daughters.

BACH

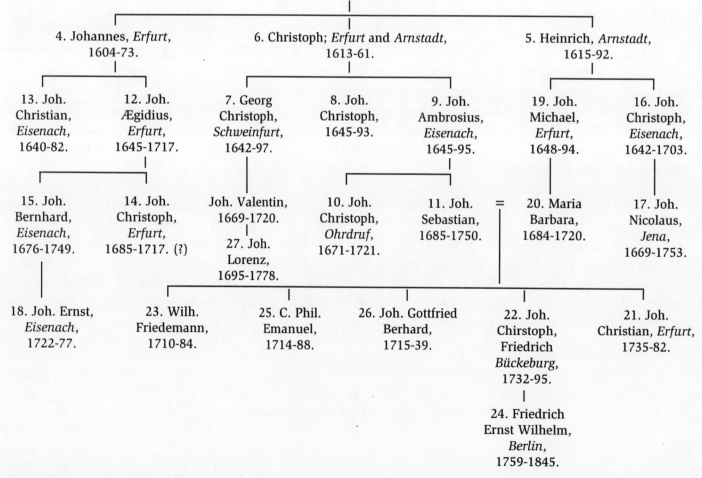

1. Hans Bach,
at *Wechmar* about 1561.

2. Veit Bach, † 1619.

3. Hans B. 'd Spielmann, † 1626.

4. Johannes, *Erfurt*, 1604-73.

6. Christoph; *Erfurt* and *Arnstadt*, 1613-61.

5. Heinrich, *Arnstadt*, 1615-92.

13. Joh. Christian, *Eisenach*, 1640-82.

12. Joh. Ægidius, *Erfurt*, 1645-1717.

7. Georg Christoph, *Schweinfurt*, 1642-97.

8. Joh. Christoph, 1645-93.

9. Joh. Ambrosius, *Eisenach*, 1645-95.

19. Joh. Michael, *Erfurt*, 1648-94.

16. Joh. Christoph, *Eisenach*, 1642-1703.

15. Joh. Bernhard, *Eisenach*, 1676-1749.

14. Joh. Christoph, *Erfurt*, 1685-1717. (?)

Joh. Valentin, 1669-1720.

27. Joh. Lorenz, 1695-1778.

10. Joh. Christoph, *Ohrdruf*, 1671-1721.

11. Joh. Sebastian, 1685-1750.

=

20. Maria Barbara, 1684-1720.

17. Joh. Nicolaus, *Jena*, 1669-1753.

18. Joh. Ernst, *Eisenach*, 1722-77.

23. Wilh. Friedemann, 1710-84.

25. C. Phil. Emanuel, 1714-88.

26. Joh. Gottfried Berhard, 1715-39.

22. Joh. Chirstoph, Friedrich *Bückeburg*, 1732-95.

21. Joh. Christian, *Erfurt*, 1735-82.

24. Friedrich Ernst Wilhelm, *Berlin*, 1759-1845.

BIBLIOGRAPHY

Editor's note:
> Every biography is based on the one written by his son Carl Phillip Emanuel and his pupil J.F. Agricola four years after his death, published by Mizler, and the one published in 1802 by Forkel.

Williams, C.F. Abdy, *Bach*
> J.M. Dent & Sons, 1934

Friedrich Blume, *Two Centuries of Bach*
> Oxford Press, 1950

Albert Schweitzer, *J.S. Bach, Vol. 1*
> MacMillan Co., Translated by Ernest Newman

Groves Dictionary of Music and Musicians
> Edited by J.A. Fuller Maitland, The MacMillan Co., 1904 (pages 142-156)

Gerhard Herz, *Bach Sources in America*
> Barenreiter Kassel Basel, 1984

the "Explication" in J. S. Bach's own handwriting.

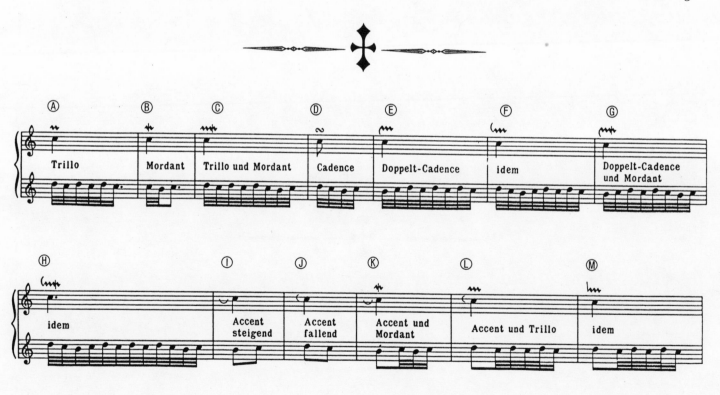

A. Trillo
B. Mordant
C. Trillo und Mordant
D. Cadence
E. Doppelt-Cadence
F. idem
G. Doppelt-Cadence und Mordant
H. idem
I. Accent steigend
J. Accent fallend
K. Accent und Mordant
L. Accent und Trillo
M. idem

MINUET IN G
from the Notebook for Anna Magdalena Bach

J. S. Bach

MINUET

from the Notebook for Anna Magdalena Bach

J. S. Bach

MINUET

Allegretto ♩. = 66

J. S. Bach

16

POLONAISE IN G

from the Notebook for Anna Magdalena Bach

J. S. Bach

MINUET IN G

from the Notebook for Wilhelm Friedemann Bach

J. S. Bach

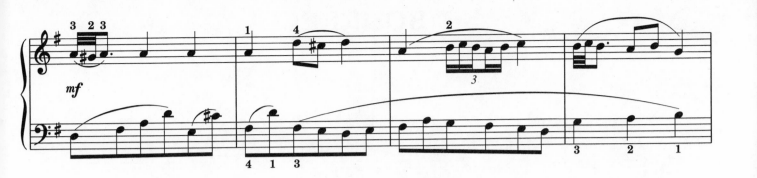

BOURRÉE

J. S. Bach

MARCH

from the Notebook for Anna Magdalena Bach

J. S. Bach

MUSETTE IN D

from the Notebook for Anna Magdalena Bach

J. S. Bach

MARCH

from the Notebook for Anna Magdalena Bach

J. S. Bach

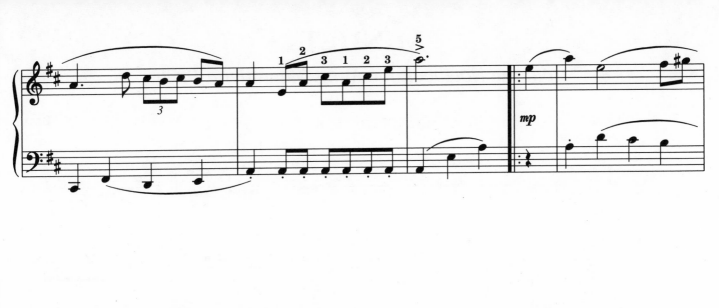

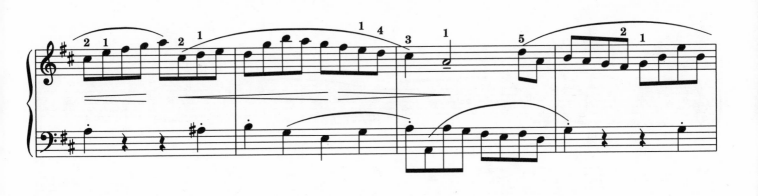

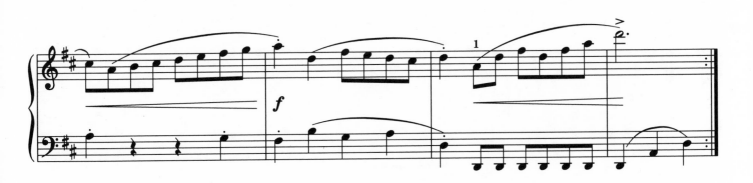

MINUET

from the Notebook for Anna Magdalena Bach

J. S. Bach

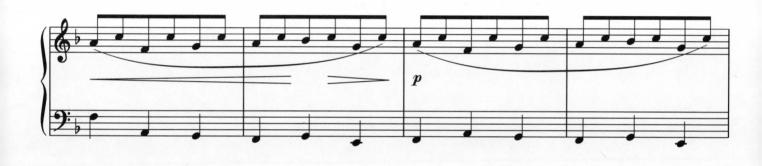

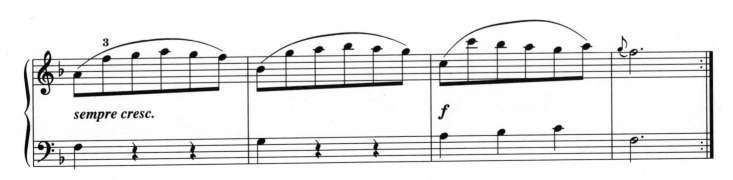

ARIA

from the Notebook for Anna Magdalena Bach

J. S. Bach

GIGUE IN F

J. S. Bach

MINUET

from the Notebook for Anna Magdalena Bach

J. S. Bach

MINUET IN G MINOR
from the Notebook for Anna Magdalena Bach

J. S. Bach

POLONAISE

from the Notebook for Anna Magdalena Bach

J. S. Bach

MINUET IN G MINOR

J. S. Bach

MINUET IN G MINOR

J. S. Bach

POLONAISE IN G MINOR

from the Notebook for Anna Magdalena Bach

J. S. Bach

Moderato energico

POLONAISE IN G MINOR

from the Notebook for Anna Magdalena Bach

J. S. Bach

MINUET IN C MINOR

from the Notebook for Anna Magdalena Bach

J. S. Bach

MINUET IN G MINOR

from the Notebook for Wilhelm Friedemann Bach

J. S. Bach

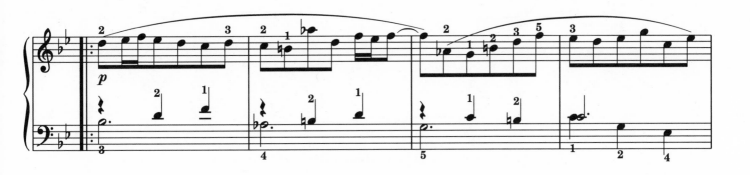

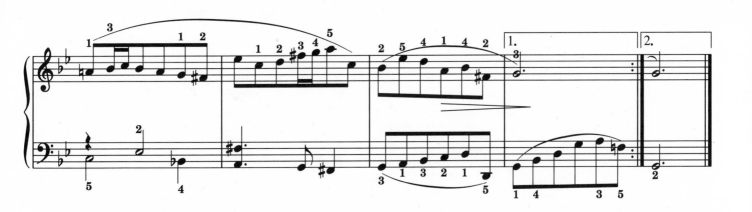

MINUET IN C MINOR

from the Notebook for Wilhelm Friedemann Bach

J. S. Bach

ALLEMANDE IN A

from the Notebook for Wilhelm Friedemann Bach

J. S. Bach

GIGUE IN A
from the Notebook for Wilhelm Friedemann Bach

J. S. Bach

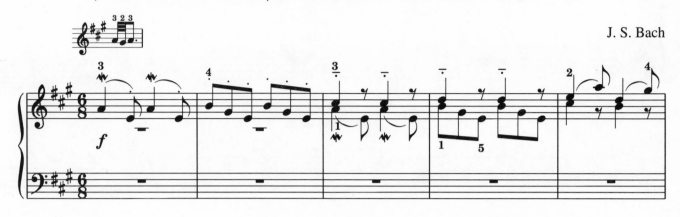

PRELUDE NO. 1 IN C

from Twelve Little Preludes for Beginners

J. S. Bach

For the convenience of Students, the embellishments in this piece were written out in smaller notes.
The following are the principal signs and the manner in which they are to be played. Ed.

a) Mordent; played:

b) Trill with slide from below; and after-beat; played:

c) Trill with slide from above, and after-beat; played:

d) Inverted Mordent; played:

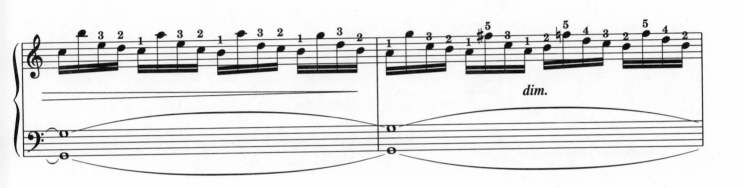

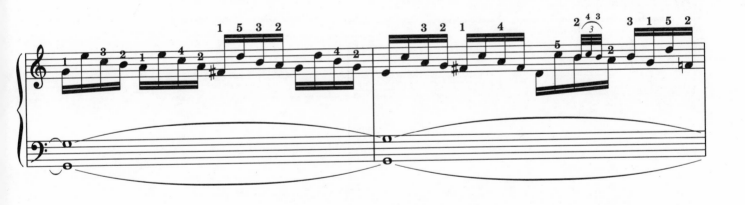

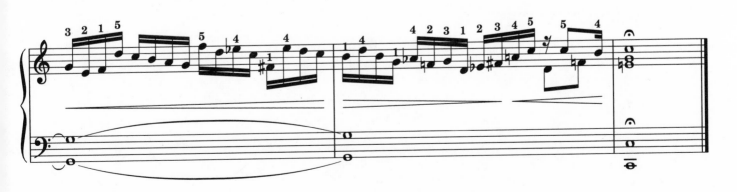

PRELUDE NO. 2 IN C

from Twelve Little Preludes for Beginners

J. S. Bach

PRELUDE NO. 3 IN C MINOR

from *Twelve Little Preludes for Beginners*

J. S. Bach

PRELUDE NO. 4 IN D

from *Twelve Little Preludes for Beginners*

J. S. Bach

PRELUDE NO. 5 IN D MINOR

from Twelve Little Preludes for Beginners

J. S. Bach

PRELUDE NO. 6 IN D MINOR

from *Twelve Little Preludes for Beginners*

J. S. Bach

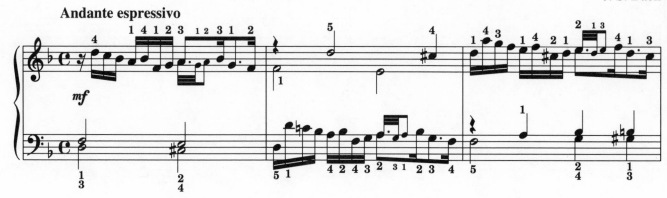

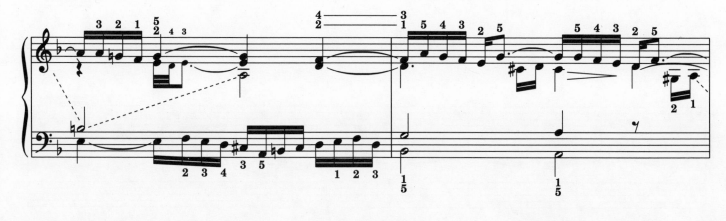

PRELUDE NO. 7 IN E MINOR

from Twelve Little Preludes for Beginners

J. S. Bach

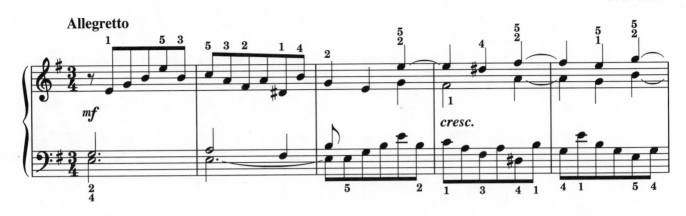

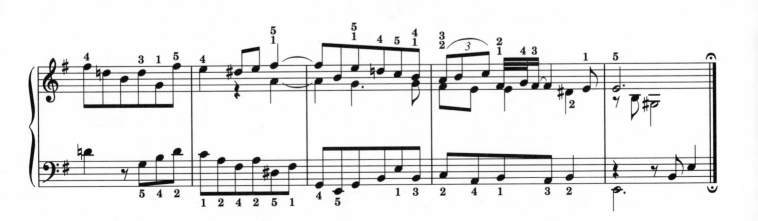

PRELUDE NO. 8 IN F

from Twelve Little Preludes for Beginners

J. S. Bach

PRELUDE NO. 9 IN F

from Twelve Little Preludes for Beginners

J. S. Bach

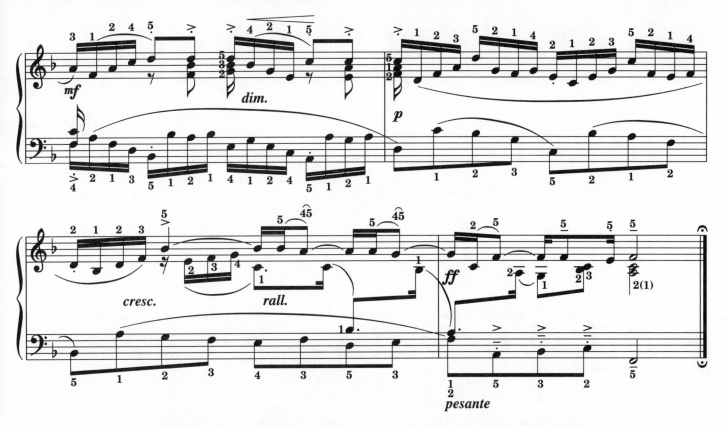

PRELUDE NO. 10 IN G MINOR

from *Twelve Little Preludes for Beginners*

J. S. Bach

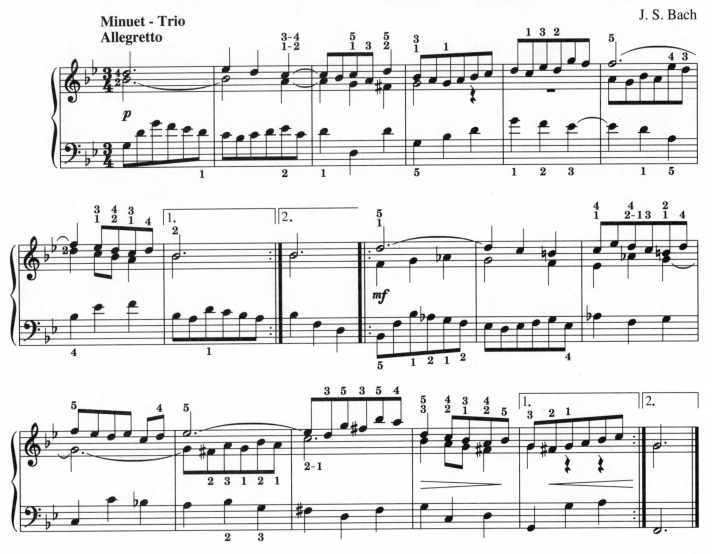

PRELUDE NO. 11 IN G MINOR

from Twelve Little Preludes for Beginners

J. S. Bach

PRELUDE NO. 12 IN A MINOR

from Twelve Little Preludes for Beginners

J. S. Bach

68

PRELUDE NO. 1 IN C

from Six Little Preludes for Beginners

J. S. Bach

PRELUDE NO. 2 IN C MINOR

from Six Little Preludes for Beginners

J. S. Bach

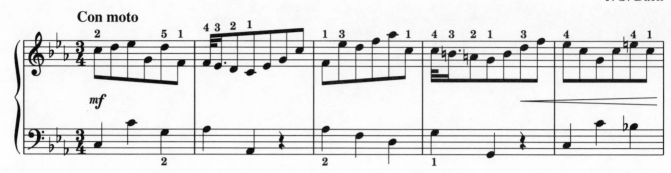

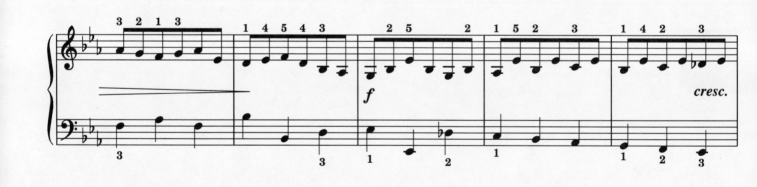

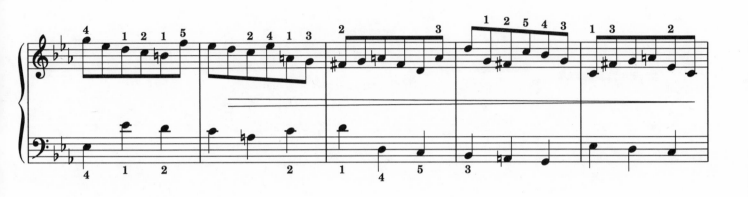

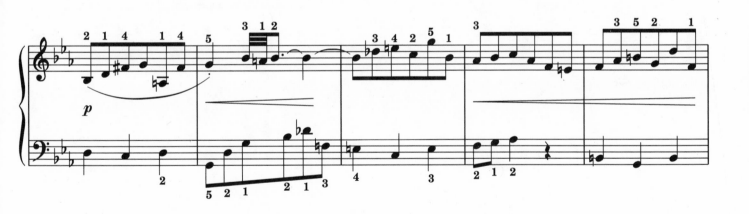

PRELUDE NO. 3 IN D MINOR

from *Six Little Preludes for Beginners*

J. S. Bach

PRELUDE NO. 4 IN D

from Six Little Preludes for Beginners

J. S. Bach

Allegretto grazioso

PRELUDE NO. 5 IN E

from Six Little Preludes for Beginners

J. S. Bach

PRELUDE NO. 6 IN E MINOR

from Six Little Preludes for Beginners

J. S. Bach

GAVOTTE

from English Suite No. 3

J. S. Bach

MUSETTE

from English Suite No. 3

J. S. Bach

Gavotte I Da Capo

PRELUDE AND FUGHETTA IN G

J. S. Bach

FUGHETTA

J. S. Bach

88

PRELUDE AND FUGHETTA IN E MINOR

J. S. Bach

Prelude
Andantino

91

FUGHETTA

PRELUDE AND FUGHETTA IN F

J. S. Bach

FUGHETTA

J. S. Bach

PRELUDE AND FUGHETTA IN D MINOR

J. S. Bach

Prelude
Sostenuto

VI

mf

FUGHETTA

PRELUDE AND FUGHETTA IN A MINOR

J. S. Bach

Prelude
Moderato

FUGHETTA

108

PRELUDE AND FUGHETTA IN E FLAT

J. S. Bach

FUGHETTA

J. S. Bach

Other Books by Gail Smith...

12 Spirituals for Piano Solo — Book
Ancient & Modern Songs of Ireland for Piano — Book & Cassette
Ancient & Modern Songs of Scotland for Piano — Book, Cassette, & CD
J. S. Bach Collection Books One - Five — Book
Beethoven Sonatas Books One - Five — Book
Celebrate the Piano 1 - 5 — Book
Classical Piano Solos for Worship Settings — Book & Cassette
Complete Book of Exercises for the Pianist — Book
Complete Book of Improvisation, Fills & Chord Progressions — Book
Complete Book of Modulations for the Pianist — Book
Complete Church Pianist — Book
Country Gospel Piano Solos — Book, Cassette, & CD
English Carols for Piano Solo — Book, Cassette, & CD
Great Literature for Piano Book 1 (Easy) — Book
Great Literature for Piano Book 2 (Elementary) — Book
Great Literature for Piano Book 3 (Intermediate) — Book
Great Literature for Piano Book 4 (Difficult) — Book
Great Literature for Piano Book 5 (More Difficult) — Book
Great Literature for Piano Book 6 (Very Difficult) — Book
Great Literature for Piano Book 7 (Advanced Sonatas) — Book
Great Literature for Piano Book 8 (Musically Advanced) — Book
Great Women Composers — Book & CD
La Fourest Piano Quartet — Book
The Life and Music of Amy Beach — Book
The Life and Music of Edward MacDowell — Book, Cassette, & CD
Native American Songs for Piano Solo — Book & CD
Opus Five/Eight Original Piano Solos — Book
Treasures from the Hymnal — Book & CD
You Can Teach Yourself® Gospel Piano — Book & CD

CREATIVE KEYBOARD PUBLICATIONS
A Division of Mel Bay Publications, Inc.
P.O. Box 66, Pacific, MO 63069-0066
1-800-8-MEL BAY (1-800-863-5229) • FAX: (636) 257-5062
Visit us on the Web at http://www.melbay.com
E-mail us at email@melbay.com

7 96279 064583

ISBN 0-7866-5027-3 >> $9.5